कARM CHAकRA

SAMAKSSHA CHAWLA

Made with ♥ on the Notion Press Platform
www.notionpress.com

Contents

Acknowledgements

This book is dedicated to the celestial guidance of Shree Krishna and the enigmatic grace of Bhairav Baba. The genesis and meticulous research that underpinned this narrative spanned several years of profound inquiry and exploration. The tapestry of this tale, woven with threads of devotion and scholarly rigor, reflects the divine inspiration and ancient wisdom imparted by these revered figures.

I am deeply indebted to my esteemed friends, Chirag and Dev, whose erudite insights and discerning perspectives significantly enriched the tapestry of this story. Their contributions have illuminated intricate facets of the narrative, infusing it with a depth and authenticity that would have otherwise remained elusive.

Furthermore, I owe a debt of gratitude to my parents, whose unwavering support and encouragement provided me with the freedom to delve deeply into the treasures of our rich and venerable culture. Their belief in the importance of preserving and understanding our cultural heritage has been a beacon guiding my research and creative endeavors.

In honoring these sources of inspiration and support, this book stands as a testament to the enduring legacy of our spiritual and cultural traditions, as well as the collaborative efforts that breathed life into its pages.

CHAPTER ONE

THE UNFORTUNATE BIRTH

Set in a parallel universe, In 2047, the world was on the verge of a new era where technology had seamlessly integrated into every aspect of human existence. Megacities sparkled with towering skyscrapers and autonomous vehicles. However, tensions simmered beneath the surface as the wealth gap widened, environmental challenges persisted, and society grappled with a blend of incredible innovation and enduring struggles.

Our story begins in Rameshwaram, a city that blends tradition and futurism. In this world, a young child named Vishnudatt faced unfortunate circumstances. Orphaned at a young age, Vishnudatt's older brothers, Vanshak and Atharvansh, struggled with the harsh realities of life. Despite this, Vishnudatt's desire to study and make a better life for himself by reaching God through the divine path of knowledge fueled a new sense of purpose in his brothers.

Initially, Vanshak was skeptical of Vishnudatt's aspirations, but eventually, he provided his younger brother with the opportunity to pursue his education, believing the lies Vishnudatt told him about using his education to lift them out of poverty.

"Here you go, bro. Study well and get us out of this hell,"

Vanshak wrote a note left on Vishnudatt's bedside table.

Vishnudatt saw this note one day and ran up to his brother, hugging him tightly. "Oh! I see you got your gift. Now study and get us out of here, okay?" Vanshak said. Vishnu nodded enthusiastically. As Vishnudatt delved into his studies, his brothers veered down a darker path, getting involved in crime and becoming increasingly hardened by their circumstances.

Despite the challenges, Vishnudatt quietly persevered, silently forced by his brothers to take on part-time work to support the household expenses while continuing his education. As the years passed, Vishnudatt's determination to reach God through his studies and the influence of his brothers' criminal activities shaped the course of their intertwined destinies.

One day, Atharvansh saw Vishnudatt taking a different path to school, which was unusual since he always took the route through the market. Suspecting that someone might be bullying him, Atharvansh followed Vishnu and saw him entering a cave on the outskirts of the city. This was very confusing as the school was on the other side of Rameshwaram. He followed Vishnudatt into the cave, trying to be as quiet as possible. After walking for another ten minutes, he saw an old man with long hair and a thick beard, wearing orange clothes and beads like a sage, sitting on an elevated stone. In front of the old man were children ranging from what looked like ten years old to twenty years old. Atharvansh faintly heard the old man's raspy voice talking about some scripture.

From what he could make out, the old man was talking about how Hanuman, Parshuram, and Ashwatthama were still alive, calling them Chiranjeevi and explaining that there are seven Chiranjeevis in the world. A hand rose, and a child asked, "Baba, what are Chiranjeevi?"

"Chiranjeevi are the immortals who roam around the world in search of the Dasa-avatar Kalki, as he will need help to defeat Kalipurush. Some became Chiranjeevi because of a curse, and some through their will," replied Vishnudatt.

"Very good, Vishnu. But, where did you get to know about that?" asked the old man.

Atharvansh's blood boiled. "He and his brother were giving him money to study so he could get them out of poverty, and this is the dumb knowledge he had been studying?" he asked himself, enraged.

He ran to his hut and told Vanshak everything.

CHAPTER TWO

FIGHTS OF FAMILY

The harsh words echoed through the thin walls of Vanshak's hut.

"Get out of here! I gave you money to study, hoping you'd lift us out of these dire circumstances! But you? You're running to that old fool, believing all that nonsense!" Vanshak's voice was thunderous with anger. From the neighboring house, an elderly woman emerged, her curiosity piqued by the commotion.

On the road, Vishnudatt's clothes and possessions were strewn haphazardly, as if they'd been thrown out in a fit of rage. Vishnudatt himself was on his knees, clutching at his older brother's feet, as Vanshak continued to berate him. "Get out of the house! Don't you ever show your face again, or I swear I'll kill you!" The old woman watched with a deep frown, her expression etched with concern and dismay.

Vishnudatt, beaten and bruised, was eventually left on the roadside. He gathered his scattered belongings and sat on a bench near a tea stall, his sobs audible even from a distance. The old woman, leaning heavily on her thin walking stick, made her way over to him, her heart aching at the sight of his bleeding elbows and knees. She instructed the tea vendor to bring a glass of milk and tea, wiping the blood off with a cloth.

"What happened, boy? Why did your brothers act in that manner?" she asked gently, her voice filled with concern.

Vishnudatt, tears streaming down his face, recounted his story between sips of milk. "My parents died when I was young. I don't even remember what my father looked like. Since then, my brothers have taken care of me in a harsh way. I tricked my older brother into believing I was studying to lift us out of poverty. But in truth, I was seeking moksha. I wandered the streets after getting admission into the public school, searching for a spiritual teacher. One day, I found a group of boys applying various tilaks—Vaishnav, Shiva, and Krishna. They changed into white dhotis and janeu before disappearing into a cave. I followed them and met a guru, whom they called 'Guru Vyas.' He seemed to know everything about me without any introduction. Yesterday, my brother Atharvansh followed me and discovered my secret, leading to the outburst you witnessed."

The old woman listened patiently, her heart going out to Vishnudatt. She helped him finish his milk and urged him to rest.

The next morning, Vishnudatt awoke to find himself still on the bench, his head resting on the old woman's lap. She was gently stroking his hair, a tender gesture of comfort. Realizing he must have cried himself to sleep, he sat up, remembering the woman's advice. Determined to follow her counsel, he made his way to the nearest bus station and inquired about the schedule. After a curt response from the supervisor, he discovered that the next bus to Kashi was at noon.

CHAPTER THREE

The Cruel Uncle

Hey! Boy! Wake up! Boy!" a brusque voice roused Vishnudatt from a scarcely earned slumber. "We are at Kashi, remit the 2000 rupees!" demanded the conductor with urgency. Vishnudatt relinquished nearly all of his savings and disembarked the bus after an arduous odyssey of 2500 km and nearly three days traversing cliffs and varied terrains.

He surveyed his surroundings, observing edifices about 50 miles distant. He discerned the chasm between affluence and destitution from the proximity of the buildings to the slum.

After perambulating a few miles, he encountered a man who appeared well-acquainted with both the city and its slums. "Hello sir, do you know where this address is?" Vishnudatt inquired, pointing to an address inscribed on a crumpled piece of paper he had found three nights prior.

"Yes, it's near the Kaal Bhairav Mandir," replied the stranger, gesturing towards an obscure street.

"Wait, gods are worshipped here?!" Vishnudatt asked, his fatigue and exhaustion seemingly dissipated by his newfound excitement as the thought of people in the city worshipping gods was out of the ordinary.

"Yes..." replied the stranger with a trace of awkwardness and perplexity.

Vishnudatt proceeded towards the street, his eyes alight with hope. After bowing at the gates of the mandir, he continued until he reached the house corresponding to the address on the paper.

The house, inspired by traditional Arab architecture, featured vibrant green walls juxtaposed with rugged, exposed brick pillars. Elegant arched windows with intricate wooden screens permitted soft, filtered light to penetrate, casting enchanting patterns within. A serene central courtyard provided a tranquil oasis. Inside, geometric patterned tiles and ornate lanterns enhanced the warm, inviting ambiance. This amalgamation of green walls, brick pillars, and arched windows created a harmonious and timeless aesthetic.

Noticing the absence of a doorbell, he opted to knock on the exquisite wooden door. As he knocked, he deliberated on how to greet his uncle, who had converted to Islam. Should he use his customary "Namaste," or "As-salaam-walekum"? He was still pondering this when the door opened, revealing a man of approximately 5'11", portly, with a long beard and orange-colored hair.

"Yes?" the man inquired with a resonant voice.

"Hello Ranbir Chacha, how are you?" asked Vishnudatt.

"Ranbir Chacha?! I don't go by that name anymore! It's Mohammed Arham now!" the man retorted indignantly.

Vishnu apologized and recounted the saga of how and why he was expelled from his home, seeking refuge and education, while concealing his true motivation for acquiring knowledge. Mohammed acquiesced to his terms with a mischievous grin. He stipulated that he would finance Vishnu's education in exchange for household chores and prohibited any part-time employment, citing the orthodoxy of Banaras in hiring a child. Vishnu reluctantly agreed, having no other kin.

The following morning, Vishnu awoke on a bench in the verandah, the space Mohammed had designated for him. Mohammed instructed him to prepare tea for everyone, using a separate cup for himself, placed near the toilet. Vishnu meticulously cleaned the cup and prepared the tea. The kitchen was diminutive and of low height. He persuaded his uncle to enroll him in school. Gradually, Vishnu acclimated to and grew resentful of his routine.

He was compelled to clean the house and toilet with his bare hands, cook for everyone, and tend to Mohammed's mother-in-law. She suffered from leg cancer, excusing her from using her legs, necessitating Vishnu's care and cleaning. He was forced to consume live insects and, on rare occasions, was left with scraps of food the family generously spared after their meals.

Despite enduring numerous cataclysmic adversities, Vishnu tenaciously upheld his ritual of frequenting the Kaal Bhairav mandir and immersing himself in the sacred waters of the Ganga each dawn. Gradually, he cultivated an intimate communion with Bhairav, ultimately discerning him as his ishta-dev.

CHAPTER FOUR

THE AGHORI'S ADVICE

During his frequent pilgrimages to the Kaal Bhairav Mandir, Vishnudatt frequently observed an enigmatic Aghori who appeared without fail on every Krishna-paksha Ashtami. This ascetic figure would remain seated throughout the day, only to disappear into the night's embrace. Driven by an insatiable curiosity, one fateful day Vishnudatt resolved to shadow the Aghori. He waited with bated breath for the baba to finish his esoteric practices and then quietly trailed him. They traversed through winding alleys and desolate pathways, the minutes stretching into what felt like hours. Eventually, the Aghori entered the foreboding precincts of a shamshan ghat, the air thick with the scent of burning pyres. Though trepidation gripped his heart, Vishnudatt gathered his courage and followed, addressing the Aghori with reverence.

"Namaste, sir. Jai Bhairav Baba. I have been observing you for many days and was wondering if you would bestow upon me the tantra diksha so that I may undertake the practices to reach Bhairav Baba," Vishnudatt implored, his voice tinged with hope.

For a long moment, the Aghori maintained an imperturbable silence. Just as despondency began to weigh upon Vishnudatt, a voice resonated through the gloom. "You are not ready yet. If you seek to traverse the tantra-marg to reach Bhairav, you must first garner the blessings of Bhairav and possess an indomitable will.

Now, elucidate to me your understanding of tantra. Do you subscribe to the banal notion of it being mere black magic?"

To Vishnudatt's astonishment, the Aghori had spoken. "No, sir," he replied with conviction. "That is abhicharkriya, a mere fragment of tantra. Tantra is the swiftest conduit to divinity, superseded only by aghor. Misconceptions abound, leading many to erroneously equate tantra with abhicharkriya due to its misrepresentation in various quarters."

Vishnudatt, known throughout Banaras for his unparalleled rendition of the Kaal Bhairav Ashtakam, remained an enigma. His origins were shrouded in mystery, but his devotional singing had earned him widespread acclaim. Days later, he returned to the Kaal Bhairav temple and once more beheld the Aghori. The same sequence of events and conversations recurred over the ensuing months. Each time, Vishnudatt faithfully followed the Aghori, reiterated his plea for tantra diksha, and received the same stoic response.

Eventually, the Aghori's patience wore thin. "I cannot confer upon you tantra-diksha or aghor-diksha," he declared. "But if your yearning for Bhairav is genuine, commence Bhairav sadhana through his naam japa. Recite the mantra 'Om Bhairavay Namah.' This simple naam mantra requires no diksha. Should Bhairav deem it so, he will guide the right teacher to you."

Vishnudatt embarked on this spiritual regimen with unwavering dedication, adhering meticulously to the Aghori's guidance. Though the Aghori did not acknowledge him as a disciple, Vishnudatt embraced him as his guru. Days bled into weeks, weeks into months, and months into years. For five long years, Vishnudatt diligently pursued his sadhana, even as he completed his 12th-grade education. His dreams and waking visions were imbued with Bhairav's presence, marked by profound signs.

One night, as Vishnudatt slumbered on his austere bench, a vision visited him. A towering shadow, approximately eight feet in height and shrouded in an impenetrable darkness, appeared. Only its glowing Shiv Tilak was discernible. A serpent coiled around its neck, and it wielded a formidable Trishul. Despite the pervasive darkness, Vishnudatt perceived a radiant light emanating from the figure, enveloping him in an ineffable peace. The shadow imparted a directive: to join the army, for that was where his destiny lay. After imparting this revelation, the shadow dissipated, and Vishnudatt awoke with a start.

Following his customary prayers and Naam Jaap, he overheard a group of young boys discussing the opening of a new recruitment office. This office, after decades of anticipation, would finally enable the local youth of Banaras to enlist in the armed forces. In that moment, Vishnudatt comprehended the import of his dream and the path he was destined to tread.

CHAPTER FIVE

NEW DICIPLINE

The soldier's voice cleaved through the early morning stillness like a clarion call, authoritative and resonant. It was a voice forged by years of rigorous discipline and unwavering duty, imbued with an intrinsic command that tolerated no delay. As it echoed through the barracks, it infused the air with an almost palpable energy, a harbinger of the day's exigent demands and expectations.

"Up and at 'em, soldiers!" he bellowed, his tone a blend of urgency and encouragement. Each syllable was enunciated with crisp precision, carrying the weight of both responsibility and camaraderie. The voice possessed a timbre that seemed to resonate within the very marrow of those it addressed, compelling an immediate and unhesitating response.

Vishnudatt's eyes flickered open, the fog of sleep swiftly dispelled by the unmistakable authority in that voice. It was a voice that carried the promise of order amidst chaos, of structure in the face of uncertainty. As the words reverberated through the room, it was as if the very walls absorbed and amplified the call to action, reinforcing its imperative nature.

"Rise and shine, let's move!" the soldier continued, the cadence of his speech steady and unwavering. There was a rhythm to his commands, a martial beat that aligned with the heartbeats of those who listened. It was not merely a call to awaken but a summons to embrace the day's mission with resolve and determination.

In the dim light of dawn, bodies stirred and stretched, the soldier's voice weaving through the air like an invisible conductor, orchestrating the synchronized movements of waking men. Each phrase, delivered with practiced assurance, guided them from the inertia of sleep to the kinetic drive of readiness. The soldier's voice, firm yet not devoid of empathy, constantly reminded them of the shared purpose and collective strength that bound them together.

Embarking on the Journey

Embarking on the journey of becoming a Gentleman Cadet (GC) in the Indian Army is akin to navigating a meticulously charted path, each step designed to metamorphose a civilian into a disciplined, resilient, and honorable military officer. Here is a detailed recounting of this transformative journey that every cadet like Vishnudatt had to endure:

The Beginning: Dawn of Discipline

0430 hours: The journey commences in the pre-dawn darkness, where the shrill call of the bugle pierces the stillness. GCs awaken from their slumber, the first rays of dawn still concealed beyond the horizon. The day begins with a surge of adrenaline as they spring from their beds, meticulously folding their blankets and donning their PT (Physical Training) attire.

The First Steps: Embracing Physical Rigors

0500 hours: The initial steps on this journey are grueling, as GCs assemble for the morning PT session. Here, they push their physical limits through a rigorous regimen of running, calisthenics, obstacle courses, and endurance exercises. Each stride and leap in the early morning mist builds the physical fortitude essential for a soldier.

Navigating Through Knowledge: Academic and Tactical Training

0630 hours: After PT, the GCs return to their barracks, where a swift transformation occurs. They change into their crisp formal uniforms, ready to tackle the intellectual challenges of the day.

0700 hours: Breakfast in the mess hall is a brief respite, providing nourishment and camaraderie before the academic pursuit commences.

0730 hours: The classrooms become the next waypoint on their journey. Here, GCs immerse themselves in a diverse curriculum, absorbing lessons in military strategy, leadership, weaponry, and general education. Each lecture and discussion serves as a stepping stone, building their theoretical understanding and strategic thinking.

1000 hours: The academic terrain yields to the practical fields, where tactical training ensues. GCs engage in drills, field exercises, and simulated combat scenarios, honing their practical skills and learning to navigate the complexities of real-life military operations.

Midday Respite and Specialized Training

1300 hours: The journey pauses for a brief respite at lunch, a time to refuel and gather strength for the afternoon ahead.

1400 hours: Post-lunch, the journey takes a more specialized turn. GCs delve into modules focused on weapon handling, map reading, navigation, and communication. These hands-on sessions are critical for mastering the intricate tools and techniques of warfare.

1600 hours: The late afternoon is reserved for sports and games, where the journey becomes a collective effort. Engaging in football, basketball, and hockey, GCs cultivate camaraderie, competitive spirit, and physical fitness, essential qualities for their future roles.

Evening Reflection and Personal Growth

1800 hours: As the sun sets, the journey allows for personal time. GCs return to their barracks to relax, shower, and attend to personal needs. This period often serves as a moment of reflection and self-study, preparing for the challenges of the next day.

1900 hours: Dinner is another waypoint where the GCs converge, sharing stories of the day and reinforcing the bonds of brotherhood.

2000 hours: The day's journey culminates with the evening roll call and daily briefings. Here, GCs gather to receive important announcements and address any concerns, ensuring everyone is aligned for the next day's path.

2100 hours: Lights out mark the end of the day's journey. The GCs retire to their bunks, weary but fulfilled, ready to embrace the challenges of the following day.

Weekend Expeditions and Celebrations

Weekends introduce different trails in the journey. They might involve additional training, cultural activities, or ceremonial parades. Occasionally, motivational lectures by senior officers or veterans offer invaluable insights and inspiration.

Festive Waypoints

During festivals and special occasions, the routine journey takes delightful detours. Celebrations, special meals, and traditional ceremonies foster a sense of unity and cultural pride among the GCs.

The Destination: Transformation into an Officer

Each day's journey in the life of a GC is a meticulously crafted expedition that melds physical rigors, intellectual pursuits, and personal growth. It instills in them the values of duty, honor, and country, preparing them to lead with courage and integrity. This arduous yet rewarding journey transmutes young cadets into proficient and honorable officers of the Indian Army, ready to navigate the vicissitudes of military life with steadfast resolve.

Despite the rigorous training, Vishnudatt did not abandon his sadhana. He persisted in chanting his mantra every single day. For two years, he received no experiences, no dreams, and no signs.

One night, as he slumbered, he heard a voice, "Don't worry, son." He couldn't open his eyes. Suddenly, he saw a vision of the same aghori in the same cremation ground. A luminous brilliance emanated from his head. A sense of bliss enveloped Vishnu in the dream as he approached the Aghori.

"Don't worry, son," the aghori said. "This is the stage where 75 percent of sadhaks and upasakas falter by abandoning their practice. If you have been experiencing visions and dreams until now and find them absent, do not despair, for this is a test that every sadhak must endure. The trial is to persistently chant."

Vishnu awoke to the soldier's firm voice once more. He followed the same routine, his resolve fortified by the vision and the sagacious words of the Aghori.

CHAPTER SIX

THE FIRST POST

Vishnudatt awoke that morning with an ineffable sense of exhilaration. The atmosphere felt different; the air carried an unfamiliar scent, and the sun's rays caressed his skin in a peculiar manner. There was an enigmatic essence in the morning that day.

Of course, it had to be. It was the inaugural day of Vishnudatt's first posting. He was assigned to Jammu-Kashmir. As a soldier, his peers would habitually rise at 4:30 AM due to rigorous conditioning, but 24-year-old Vishnu would awake at 3:00 AM sharp for his sadhana.

This routine became an immutable part of Vishnu's life. As the years elapsed, he became an integral part of the mountains, assimilating their stoic presence. Many of his peers attempted to dissuade him from his sadhana, but Vishnu remained resolute. One day, a fellow soldier approached him, "Hey Vishnu! How are you?"

"I am fine, thank you, Ashatham. How is your jappa progressing?" Vishnu inquired with a courteous tone.

"Amazing! I achieved my target of 100,000 recitations and had an incredible vision last night!" Ashatham exclaimed.

"Good! Now prepare yourself for the pisach test, my friend," Vishnu replied. Ashatham nodded and then inquired about Vishnu's jappa.

"I reached 1,600,000 recitations the day before yesterday," Vishnu responded.

Ashatham, intrigued, asked why Vishnu had not moved on to the next stage of his spiritual journey despite reaching such a significant milestone. Vishnu had no answer to offer. He found himself in a quandary, pondering what was transpiring in his life and what steps he should take to unlock the next path.

He applied for a three-day leave and was granted permission. Ascending one of the hills, isolated from the town, he immersed himself in continuous jappa, hoping for a sign to illuminate his path. He abstained from eating, sleeping, drinking, or performing any daily activity, focusing solely on his meditation. He entered a trance-like state, losing all conception of time. This profound meditation connected him to a state of bliss reminiscent of an experience he once had in Kashi.

In this state, he heard a familiar voice repeatedly utter the words, "Ma Kamakhya anushthan." Startled, he emerged from his meditation with a newfound purpose for his spiritual progress and growth.

The next morning, he returned to the camp. "Vishnudatt?! Vishnudatt?!" called the postmaster in the office.

"Here you go, this is for you," the postmaster said, handing him a letter before departing.

24/07/2071

Captain Vishnudatt

Regimental Barracks,

Jammu,

Indian Army

Subject: Transfer Order to Shambala

Dear Captain Vishnudatt,

I hope this letter finds you in good health and high spirits. It is with great pride and a sense of responsibility that I convey the following orders, issued under my authority as Commanding Officer.

Under the operational requirements and strategic needs of our regiment, you are hereby transferred to the esteemed post at Shambala, effective immediately. This transfer is a testament to your exemplary service, unwavering dedication, and the distinguished conduct you have consistently demonstrated in your current assignment.

Shambala, known for its unique and challenging terrain, requires the acumen and resilience of officers like yourself. Your proven leadership skills, tactical proficiency, and ability to inspire and command respect among your peers make you an ideal candidate for this critical position.

Details of your new assignment are as follows:

Reporting Date: [30/7/2071]

Reporting Officer: Brigadier Arunesh Singh

Location: Shambala Base Camp, Assam

Upon receipt of this letter, you are instructed to make the necessary arrangements to complete the handover of your current duties and responsibilities. Coordination with your current commanding officer is essential to ensure a smooth transition. Additionally, please liaise with the logistics department to facilitate the transfer of your personal and professional belongings to Shambala.

Your presence at Shambala is expected to bolster our operational capabilities and further the strategic objectives of our regiment and the Indian Army as a whole. We have full confidence in your abilities to undertake and excel in this new assignment.

Should you require any assistance or further clarification regarding your transfer, please do not hesitate to contact the Personnel Affairs Office via email at personnel.affairs@indianarmy.gov.in.

We commend your continuous commitment to serving our nation and trust that you will bring the same level of excellence and dedication to your new post. May your tenure at Shambala be marked with success and fulfillment.

Wishing you all the very best in your future endeavors.

Jai Hind!

Yours sincerely,

Colonel Rajveer Singh

Commanding Officer
Jat Regiment
Indian Army

Upon reading this, Vishnudatt did not experience the disquietude that often accompanies such news. Instead, he felt elated. He knew that the Kamakhya Temple was in Assam, near Shambala. He interpreted this transfer as an unequivocal sign from Bhairav.

CHAPTER SEVEN

FIRST LOVE

After an arduous journey spanning an entire day, the weary Vishnudatt was introduced to a Subedar. "Good morning, sir!" said the Subedar in a voice that was firm yet mellifluous. "I hope you had a comfortable journey, sir. Your quarters are prepared."

"Thank you, but may I inquire your name, kind gentleman?" Vishnudatt asked, his curiosity piqued.

The Subedar, with an air of modest authority, introduced himself as Harihom Pratap. Upon reaching his quarters, Vishnudatt took a moment to compose himself before reporting to the commanding officer. "Good afternoon, sir! I am Vishnudatt, recently posted from Kashi to Kamakhya. I serve in the Jatt Regiment."

The commanding officer Brigadier Arunesh Singh greeted him with a stern yet welcoming demeanor. "Welcome to Shambala, Vishnu. Now freshen up; it is time for lunch." Vishnudatt acknowledged the command and returned to his quarters to prepare himself.

In the mess hall, Vishnudatt selected a plate and perused the array of culinary delights. Today's spread featured rajma, kali-daal, matar-paneer, butter chicken, rice, and roti. He chose a bit of everything and seated himself at a table. As he savored his meal, his thoughts meandered towards the anushthan. Suddenly, his gaze locked with that of a girl who had been observing him. She possessed eyes like emeralds, long, thick, curly hair, thin lips, and a button nose. Her short stature and hourglass figure rendered her an ethereal vision. All thoughts vanished as Vishnudatt was captivated by her presence.

They continued to gaze at each other until a comrade sat down beside Vishnudatt. Sumathi staring into Vishnudatt's grey deep eyes, and Vishnudatt staring into the dark blue eyes of Sumathi.

"She is Sumathi. Everyone boy is in love with her , but she seldom reciprocates their attentions," the comrade remarked.

Vishnudatt blushed and reluctantly tore his eyes away from her. "Really?! What is she like?"

"Wow, not even asking my name," the comrade teased. "Well, Sumathi is a spirited and courageous woman from what I understand. With unwavering determination and sharp intellect, she rapidly ascended through the ranks. Her eyes, imbued with the fire of patriotism, often soften when she gazes at the mountains, finding solace in their silent strength. Oh, and my name is Ishwar Singh."

Their second encounter was markedly less romantic. During a routine patrol, Vishnudatt, unfamiliar with the rugged terrain, stumbled and fell. Sumathi, leading the patrol, swiftly came to his aid. As she helped him to his feet, their eyes met, and in that fleeting moment, a silent understanding was forged. Sumathi gazed upon vishnudatt's curly hair and sharp features. They shared an unspoken recognition of the battles each fought, both on the field and within themselves.

As days melted into weeks, their interactions became more frequent. Sumathi admired Vishnudatt's unwavering dedication and his ability to remain composed under pressure. Vishnudatt, in turn, was drawn to Sumathi's fiery spirit and relentless pursuit of excellence. They began sharing stories of their pasts, their aspirations, and the burdens they bore.

One evening, beneath the starlit expanse of Shambala, Sumathi and Vishnudatt found themselves on the base's rooftop, a sanctuary they both frequented for quiet reflection. The night air was cold, but the stars glittered with a celestial brilliance, casting a gentle glow over the rugged landscape.

"Do you ever ponder the future?" Sumathi asked, her voice barely a whisper against the night.

Vishnudatt turned to her, his eyes mirroring the stars she observed. "I do," he responded. "But I've learned to cherish the present. Especially moments like these."

Sumathi smiled, feeling an inner warmth that defied the chill. She squeezed Vishnu's hand in hers "I'm glad we met, Vishnu. I feel I can put my guard down when I am around you."

He went closer to Sumathi. Pushing her hair behind her ear gently. "And I feel the same, Sumathi. In this world of uncertainty, you have become my person."

Under the dark sky of the night with twinkling stars. The two lovebirds shared a kiss of love.

From that night onward, their bond deepened. They became each other's confidants, their love blossoming amid the trials and tribulations of military life. They found joy in simple pleasures—a shared meal, a stroll in the mountains, a silent conversation beneath the stars.

Their love story was not devoid of challenges. The unpredictability of their duty, prolonged separations, and omnipresent danger tested their relationship. Yet, Sumathi and Vishnudatt understood that their love was worth the struggle. They drew strength from each other, facing every obstacle with unwavering support and understanding.

Years passed, and their love only grew stronger. Sumathi and Vishnudatt continued to serve their country with pride, but now, they did so with the comforting knowledge that they were never alone. They had discovered their home in each other, a love as resilient and enduring as the mountains of Shambala.

CHAPTER EIGHT

ANUSHTHAN

Captain Vishnudatt stood at attention outside the commanding officer's office, his heart pounding with a mix of determination and apprehension. The air was thick with anticipation as he took a deep breath, steeling himself for the conversation ahead. He knocked briskly on the heavy wooden door, the sound echoing through the quiet corridor.

"Come in," came the firm but familiar voice from inside.

Opening the door with a measured precision, Vishnudatt stepped in and saluted sharply. "Good morning, Sir."

Brigadier Arunesh Singh, the commanding officer, looked up from his paperwork and smiled, the corners of his eyes crinkling. "Good morning, Captain. What can I do for you?"

Vishnudatt advanced with purposeful strides, stopping before the brigadier's imposing mahogany desk. "Sir, I'd like to discuss my leave application."

"Of course," Rajan said, gesturing to the chair opposite him. "Have a seat."

Vishnudatt lowered himself into the chair, maintaining an upright posture, his hands resting on his knees with an almost statuesque stillness. "Sir, I am requesting a month's leave."

Brigadier Singh raised an inquisitive eyebrow, leaning back in his chair thoughtfully. "A month, you say? That's quite a substantial amount of time. What's the reason for your leave?"

Vishnudatt drew a deep breath, his resolve unwavering. “Sir, it’s for personal reasons. I’ve ensured that my duties will be covered in my absence.”

The next morning, after meticulously briefing the second-in-command for the last time, he departed the premises. The dawn air was crisp and filled with the promise of his impending journey. He kissed his beautiful wife, Sumathi, whose eyes reflected a blend of pride and concern. Disguised in the austere attire of a sadhu, adorned with rudraksha malas, he carried an axe, samagri, some ghee, and water bottles. Each item was chosen with deliberate care.

For three arduous days, he traversed rugged terrains, his destination a solitary mountain peak, isolated enough to remain undisturbed.

Upon arrival, he methodically cut down a nearby tree, the rhythmic sound of his axe striking the wood echoing through the wilderness. From the thick, fibrous bark, he fashioned planks, carrying them to the summit where he intended to perform a havan. With reverence, he took a handful of water and solemnly stated his name, address, gotra, and all requisite details before allowing the water to seep into the ground, thus initiating the anushthan for Ma Kamakhya.

He seated himself in meditation, his body immovable, as if hewn from stone. For 27 days, he remained steadfast, plunging into depths of meditation so profound that time itself seemed to dissolve. This was the third time he had reached such a transcendent state on his spiritual journey. After ten days of ceaseless chanting, his mantra resonating through 240 hours, he perceived a sign within his meditation, an affirmation that the anushthan was progressing favorably. A profound sense of happiness surged through his being.

Ultimately, after 27 days and approximately 650 hours of relentless japa, he was graced with a darshan of Ma Kamakhya. Her ethereal presence radiated a divine brilliance that enveloped him. "I am pleased by your dedication and practice. Ask what you want, child," Ma Kamakhya intoned, her voice resonant with celestial harmony.

Vishnudatt, his heart swelling with devotion, replied, "I just want to know what I should do next to reach Bhairav."

"Go back to your wife and keep faith in bhairav and your wife, my child" Ma Kamakhya instructed, her words imbued with an omnipotent certainty.

Vishnudatt nodded in acquiescence, basking in the sublime radiance and sense of bliss emanating from her presence, wholly surrendering to her divine will. As he concluded his havan, Ma Kamakhya's form dissipated into the ether, leaving behind an aura of profound serenity.

Upon returning home, he navigated the familiar pathways with a newfound tranquility. He made his way to the shower, the cascading water washing away the remnants of his arduous pilgrimage. Freshened up, he joined his wife at the table, the sight of the delicious lunch she had prepared evoking a deep sense of gratitude and contentment.

CHAPTER NINE

THE NEW GUEST

Vishnudatt was sitting on the porch of their small, cozy home, lost in his thoughts as the sun began to set. The golden hues bathed the surroundings in a warm glow, and he found solace in the gentle breeze that rustled through the trees. It had been a long day at work, and he was looking forward to a quiet evening with Sumathi.

Inside, Sumathi stood in front of the bathroom mirror, staring at the small plastic device in her hand. Her heart raced as she saw the two pink lines that confirmed what she had suspected for days. She was pregnant. A rush of emotions washed over her – joy, excitement, and a hint of anxiety about how Vishnudatt would react.

Taking a deep breath, she stepped out of the bathroom and walked toward the porch. She found Vishnudatt, his silhouette framed by the setting sun. She hesitated for a moment, gathering her courage, before calling his name.

"Vishnu?"

He turned to her, his face lighting up with a warm smile. "Sumathi, come join me. The sunset is beautiful tonight."

Sumathi walked over and sat beside him, taking his hand in hers. "Vishnu, there's something I need to tell you."

Her serious tone made his smile fade slightly, replaced by a look of concern. "What is it, Sumathi? Is everything okay?"

She nodded, squeezing his hand. "Yes, everything is fine. In fact, it's more than fine. Vishnu, I'm pregnant."

For a moment, there was silence. Vishnudatt's eyes widened in surprise, and he opened his mouth to speak but no words came out. He looked into Sumathi's eyes, searching for confirmation that this was real.

"Pregnant?" he finally managed to say, his voice a mix of wonder and disbelief. "Are you sure?"

Sumathi nodded, tears of joy welling up in her eyes. "Yes, I took the test twice to be sure. We're going to have a baby, Vishnu."

A slow smile spread across Vishnudatt's face, growing wider with each passing second. He pulled Sumathi into a tight embrace, his heart pounding with happiness. "A baby... We're going to be parents!" he exclaimed, his voice filled with joy.

Sumathi laughed through her tears, feeling a weight lift off her shoulders. "Yes, Vishnu. We're going to be parents."

Vishnudatt pulled back slightly, looking at her with a mixture of excitement and protectiveness. "How are you feeling? Are you okay? Do you need anything?"

She smiled, touched by his immediate concern. "I'm feeling good, just a little tired. But I'll be fine. I have you with me."

Vishnudatt cupped her face in his hands, his eyes shining with love. "I'll be here every step of the way, Sumathi. We'll do this together. I'll take care of you and our baby."

Over the next few weeks, Vishnudatt threw himself into preparing for their new arrival. He accompanied Sumathi to every doctor's appointment, asked endless questions to ensure she was healthy, and started planning the nursery. His protective nature kicked into high gear, and he was constantly by her side, making sure she had everything she needed.

One evening, as they sat together looking through baby name books, Vishnudatt took Sumathi's hand in his. "I never imagined I could be this happy," he said softly. "You've given me a gift I never thought possible."

Sumathi leaned her head on his shoulder, feeling a deep sense of contentment. "And you've given me the best partner I could ever ask for. Our baby is lucky to have you as a father."

As the months passed, their anticipation grew, and so did their love for each other. Vishnudatt's initial surprise had blossomed into a profound joy, and he embraced his new role with open arms. They faced the journey of pregnancy together, supporting each other through the highs and lows, knowing that the arrival of their child would bring even more love and happiness into their lives.

Their journey had only just begun, but they knew that whatever the future held, they would face it together, their love and their new family guiding them every step of the way

CHAPTER TEN

POSSESSIONS

"Pandit ji, can you please provide a raksha dhaga for our forthcoming progeny?" beseeched Vishnudatt to the venerable Pandit of the Bhairav Mandir adjacent to his abode.

"Indeed, it is within my capacity to bestow such protection. However, I shall require the child's kundali. Thus, return when the newborn graces this world," responded the Pandit with an air of sagacity.

Acquiescing with a nod, Vishnudatt departed for a quaint café, accompanied by his gravid wife, who was six months along. The air was redolent with the aroma of freshly brewed coffee, mingling with the subtler scents of baked pastries.

"Hey! Vishnu, how are you, brother?" a familiar baritone voice punctuated the ambient chatter, diverting Vishnudatt's attention from his steaming cup. None other than Ishwar Singh, his bosom friend, approached with his family in tow.

The tables were amalgamated, and the ensuing camaraderie was effervescent and nostalgic. Hours melted away in jocular exchanges and affectionate reminiscences, the café buzzing with the convivial energy of reunited companions.

As the conviviality came to its inevitable conclusion, both families extricated themselves from the warm embrace of the café's ambiance.

"Farewell, brother," Ishwar intoned, his voice imbued with genuine warmth. Vishnudatt reciprocated with an embrace imbued with heartfelt affection.

However, as they ambulated towards their domicile, an ominous detonation of a blast reverberated through the air near the town hall. Pivoting, Vishnudatt beheld a harrowing sight: the dreaded black army, an enigmatic leader rumored to be under the dominion of a demonic influence, had besieged their town.

Pandemonium ensued as Vishnudatt and Ishwar, clutching their families close, sprinted towards the sanctity of the protected bunkers. The malevolence of the black army was palpable, as they ravaged, pillaged, and desecrated the once serene city. Amidst the cacophony of destruction, a pernicious dread settled upon the beleaguered citizens.

In the midst of the chaos, a horrifying realization struck Vishnudatt—his beloved wife was missing. Frantically scanning the tumultuous scene, his eyes locked onto a heart-wrenching tableau: his wife, lying in a puddle of her own blood, her life force ebbing away. A visceral scream escaped his lips, "SUMI!" as he dashed towards her, Ishwar following Vishnudatt , only to be felled by a bullet.

Despite the peril, Vishnudatt mustered Herculean strength to drag his wounded wife into a nearby alley, his heart wracked with anguish as he endeavored to rouse her. The ferocity of the assault eventually waned, and Vishnudatt emerged from the alley, only to be confronted by the ghastly sight of Ishwar's lifeless form, surrounded by his grieving family.

Averting his gaze, Vishnudatt's eyes fell upon the idol of Bhairav Baba from the mandir, standing serenely amidst the devastation.

"Why? ... Why?!" A keening wail of despair erupted from Vishnudatt's soul. "You, who are venerated and feared, could not protect her?! From the moment of my birth, you have bestowed nothing but tribulations upon me! Not a single respite of happiness! You have claimed my parents, torn my family apart, turned my brothers against me, condemned me to a life of servitude, forced me to subsist on insects, and now, when I had found a friend, a wife, when I glimpsed a modicum of joy... you snatched it away. YOU

TOOK IT!"

The vehemence of his accusations reverberated through the desolate streets, his lamentations raw and unrestrained. Ishwar's family staring at Vishnudatt"This is the recompense for my unwavering devotion, for my sadhna in your name?! I shall obliterate you! I shall annihilate you, Bhairav!"

Blinded by incandescent rage, Vishnudatt barreled into the partially destroyed library. He voraciously amassed an eclectic collection of arcane spiritual tomes and esoteric scriptures, retreating into a secluded room. Whispers proliferated throughout the town, each iteration more fantastical than the last. The populace believed Vishnudatt had engaged in nefarious black magic practices within his self-imposed confinement, with dire consequences for any who ventured near.

Only one soul dared approach the sanctum of his seclusion—a young boy named Raj, who surreptitiously delivered food and water to the tormented man each day, driven by an inscrutable blend of curiosity and trepidation.

CHAPTER ELEVEN

THE ISOLATING DARSHAN

"Om tara divyahe namah." As Vishnudatt sank deeper into his meditation, an evocative vision emerged before him: a desolate samshan ghat, where a familiar, enigmatic figure appeared—the Aghori who had previously guided him to recite the Bhairav Naamah mantra said this mantra.

"What good did your adesh do?! He doesn't manifest before me, cannot safeguard my loved ones, and has stripped me of everything!" Vishnudatt's voice trembled with fury and sorrow.

"You are destined for great things, Vishnu," replied the Aghori, his tone imbued with an ancient wisdom.

"How? By taking away the only people who loved me?!" Vishnudatt's despair was palpable, his words cutting through the stillness like a blade. Despite the Aghori's attempts at consolation, Vishnudatt's anguish was impervious.

The Aghori, undeterred, presented Vishnudatt with a beej mantra dedicated to Ma Kali. "Perform this sadhna now, my child. You have devoted yourself to Bhairav long enough; he will guide and assist you in this new path."

"I do not require his aid! I am fully capable on my own!" Vishnudatt retorted vehemently.

As he concluded his vehement protest, he emerged from his meditation and commenced reading the the scriptures. Over the course of a year, he immersed himself in rigorous tantrik practices, adhering to a variety of mantra sadhanas as prescribed by the Aghori.

On the night of Krishna Paksha Ashtami, Vishnudatt emerged from his seclusion, transformed beyond recognition with his unkempt beard and wild hair. Clad in an orange dhoti and adorned with rudraksha beads, he embarked on a formidable journey toward the towering mountain that loomed over Shambala. The townspeople, including a face that sparked whispered speculation, watched in awe as he set forth, but Vishnudatt, absorbed in his determined quest, remained oblivious.

Guided by an imperceptible presence—the Aghori, his spiritual mentor—Vishnudatt braved perilous terrain, traversing dense forests and harsh landscapes on his path to Tibet. The Aghori's guidance, manifested through subtle omens and cryptic counsel, directed Vishnudatt through this grueling expedition.

Upon reaching the base of a majestic, snow-clad mountain in Tibet, Vishnudatt ventured into its glacial depths, driven by his relentless quest. After navigating through labyrinthine ice tunnels for days, he arrived at a vast chamber illuminated by an otherworldly glow. There, he encountered Hanuman, resplendent and majestic.

Vishnudatt fell to his knees, overwhelmed by a complex mixture of reverence and persistent fury. He poured out his grief and anger, seeking answers and resolution. Hanuman, embodying a serene presence and profound wisdom, listened with an unwavering calm. Despite Hanuman's gentle, persuasive attempts to sway Vishnudatt towards reconsidering his vendetta against Bhairav, Vishnudatt's resolve remained unshaken. Recognizing the futility of confrontation, Hanuman declined to align himself with Vishnudatt's cause, his refusal marked by an air of compassionate authority.

CHAPTER TWELVE

The Knowledge Of......

Hanuman offered Vishnudatt a different path, one that diverged from confrontation. With his wisdom, Hanuman suggested seeking out the legendary figure Parshuram, believed to dwell in the spectral remains of a once-thriving town in the Kashmir region. Hanuman's guidance was unequivocal—though he would not assist directly in Vishnudatt's quest against Bhairav, he could point him toward Parshuram, whose profound wisdom might illuminate a new course of action.

With Hanuman's counsel resonating in his mind, Vishnudatt embarked on the arduous journey to Kashmir. The trek was fraught with perils and challenges, each step drawing him deeper into the heart of desolation. The air was thick with the echoes of a forgotten past, and the landscape was strewn with the remnants of a bygone era, a poignant reminder of the town's erstwhile glory.

As Vishnudatt neared the abandoned town, the gravity of his journey weighed heavily upon him. The silence was almost palpable, a ghostly testament to the town's previous vibrancy. Among the ruins, Vishnudatt could sense the enigmatic presence of Parshuram, a spectral beacon guiding him through the forsaken streets.

The search led Vishnudatt to a secluded hermitage on the outskirts of the desolate town. This hermitage, though modest, emanated an aura of profound tranquility and ancient wisdom. It was here, in this sanctified haven, that Vishnudatt finally encountered Parshuram. The sage, despite his age, radiated an aura of strength and serenity, his presence imbued with an ageless wisdom.

Parshuram welcomed Vishnudatt with a discerning gaze and a serene demeanor, listening intently to the tale of turmoil and rage that had propelled Vishnudatt to this point. However, adhering to the Aghori's advice, Vishnudatt chose to conceal his true motives. He approached Parshuram with deference, expressing an earnest desire to learn the ancient knowledge of astras and shastras.

Recognizing the fervent determination and potential within Vishnudatt, Parshuram agreed to take him under his tutelage. Over the next two years, Vishnudatt immersed himself in rigorous study, absorbing the intricate details of the astras and shastras. The knowledge he sought was profound and extensive, typically requiring decades to master. Yet, Vishnudatt's unwavering dedication and relentless focus allowed him to assimilate this sacred wisdom at an accelerated pace.

Parshuram's teachings encompassed not only the physical aspects of the astras but also their spiritual significance and the ethical imperatives of their use. Vishnudatt learned about the cosmic balance, the delicate interplay between wrath and wisdom, and the paramount importance of inner peace. The sage's guidance was subtle yet transformative, leading Vishnudatt to a deeper understanding of his quest.

Without being aware of the veiled motives behind Vishnudatt's pursuit, Parshuram concentrated on imparting the divine wisdom that Vishnudatt sought, trusting that true enlightenment would emerge from the knowledge bestowed. The rigorous training demanded both intellectual acumen and spiritual growth, reshaping Vishnudatt's perspective and preparing him for the challenges that lay ahead.

After two intense years of study, Vishnudatt had undergone a profound transformation. From a grief-stricken seeker of vengeance, he had evolved into a scholar armed with divine knowledge and weapons and a deeper comprehension of cosmic principles. Parshuram's teachings provided him with a solid foundation, equipping him with the tools to confront his quest with newfound clarity and power.

As Vishnudatt prepared to continue his journey, fortified by the wisdom imparted by Parshuram, he felt a sense of balance and purpose, still blinded with the rage and fire of taking revenge against the god.

CHAPTER THIRTEEN

TARA-PITH SAMSHAN

"Go to the Tara Ma Maha Shamshan," the voice of the Aghori reverberated in Vishnudatt's ears on his pilgrimage to Kashi. By now, he was accustomed to the Aghori's ethereal manner of communication, each directive arriving with an uncanny clarity. Without hesitation, Vishnudatt altered his course from Kashi to Bengal, undertaking an arduous three-day journey through diverse and challenging terrains on foot.

Upon arriving at the periphery of the ghat, the Tara Ma Maha Shamshan Ghat revealed itself as a liminal realm, poised delicately between the corporeal and the celestial. It was an ancient, enigmatic necropolis, saturated with the gravity of millennia and imbued with a tangible aura of the supernatural. The ghat unfurled along the serpentine banks of a silvery, sinuous river that shimmered faintly under the ghostly pallor of the moonlight, casting eldritch reflections on its serene surface.

The ground was strewn with the vestiges of innumerable pyres, their ashes amalgamating with the dust of antiquity, crafting a spectral topography of ashen grays and ghostly whites. The atmosphere was thick with the cloying aroma of incense, intermingled with the acrid tang of smoldering wood, bestowing upon the place a paradoxical ambiance of sanctity and disquiet. Worn stone pathways, polished smooth by the ceaseless passage of countless feet, meandered towards the central sanctum dedicated to Tara Ma, the venerable god of the ghat.

The shrine was a venerable edifice, its somber stone carvings depicting cosmic skirmishes and celestial entities in exquisite detail. The flickering luminescence of numerous oil lamps cast capricious shadows on the walls, suffusing the surroundings with a preternatural glow. Encircling the area were dense, umbral woods, their towering trees murmuring arcane secrets in the susurrus of the wind.

Above, the sky unfurled as a vast tapestry of profound indigo, bespeckled with stars that appeared disconcertingly proximate, as if they might descend to bear witness to the rituals below. Sporadic gusts of wind disturbed the pervasive stillness, carrying with them the distant echoes of chants and the soft, mournful intonations of ritualistic supplications. The overall atmosphere was one of haunting veneration, a locus where the boundary between existence and oblivion was tenuous, and where the divine and the mortal coexisted in a fragile, enigmatic equilibrium.

Vishnudatt entered the shamshan ghat, feeling the numinous presence of Tara Ma permeating the air. He perambulated slowly around the Tara-pith, observing the occasional conflagration of corpses with a reverent detachment. He gravitated towards a solitary tree, conspicuously set apart from the rest of the ghat. As he seated himself beneath its boughs, his eyes involuntarily closed, and the Aghori materialized before him.

"From now on, you will enter into a state of samadhi," the Aghori intoned, his voice suffused with a solemn gravity. "I shall not reveal the duration of this state, but know that you will attain an unparalleled degree of spiritual evolution within a remarkably brief span. Adhere unwaveringly to my guidance, and you shall ascend to the highest states of sadhna."

Vishnudatt, with an implicit nod of assent and trust, acceded to the Aghori's pronouncement. He surrendered himself to the profound stillness, prepared to embark on a transcendental journey of inner transformation

CHAPTER FOURTEEN

TIME

As Vishnudatt settled into his meditative padmasana posture, the Aghori began the solemn rite. He whispered potent mantras into the still air, each syllable imbued with the ancient puissance of the gods. These mantras, a sacred lexicon, were uttered in a cadence that resonated deep within Vishnudatt's soul, unraveling the mundane bindings of his earthly existence.

Time became an abstract concept, losing its conventional grip on Vishnudatt's consciousness. The days turned into weeks, weeks into months, and months into years. The Aghori, ever vigilant, would intermittently bestow upon Vishnudatt the mantras of different deities. Each mantra was like a key, unlocking new realms of spiritual understanding and transcendence. The invocations ranged from the fierce and protective chants of Kali Ma to the serene and omnipotent hymns of Vishnu. These mantras reverberated through the cavern, creating a tapestry of divine sound that wrapped around Vishnudatt's being, fortifying his resolve and deepening his samadhi.

Vishnudatt remained ensconced in a state of divine absorption. His physical form, sustained by the spiritual energy of the mantras, became a vessel of profound tranquility and insight. His beard grew even longer, his hair wilder, but his countenance was one of serene enlightenment, a reflection of the divine truths he had internalized.

Then, one fateful day, the Aghori approached Vishnudatt, his presence a tangible shift in the ghat's atmosphere. With a voice that seemed to emanate from the very depths of the earth, the Aghori spoke, his words laden with the gravity of destiny. He declared that the time had come for Vishnudatt to emerge from his samadhi. The command was not merely a directive but a profound cosmic decree, echoing the authority of the divine.

As Vishnudatt slowly roused from his deep meditative state, his eyes fluttered open, revealing a gaze that seemed to pierce through the veil of reality itself. The Aghori told him to undertake an anushthan of one year with the most intense rules he could conduct. Under the instructions of the Aghori, Vishnudatt made his way to a dhuni and commenced the anushthan of Ma Tara.

After initiating his anushthan, he made his way back to the dead tree, astonished by what the world had become—a desolate wasteland, plagued by sandstorms and echoes of screams and suffering of the have-nots, juxtaposed with the laughter of the rich and pervasive cruelty and harm.

As Vishnudatt sat down and went into samadhi, he set the rules of the anushthan. As his consciousness delved deeper, guided by the spectral presence of his Aghori mentor, he began to transcend the earthly realm. His journey through the celestial spheres commenced, thanks to the anushthan each plane a step closer to his ultimate goal: Shiva Lok, the abode of Lord Shiva. This was not a journey of passive observation but one of active conquest, driven by a burning vendetta.

CHAPTER FIFTEEN

THE FINAL ASCEND

First, he traversed Indraloka, the realm of the gods ruled by Indra. Here, the air shimmered with divine light, and the celestial beings moved with an ethereal grace. Vishnudatt, with his mind honed by years of rigorous spiritual practice, approached the gods not with reverence, but with resolute determination. The Devas, sensing his intention, tried to counsel him, their voices resonant with divine wisdom and concern. They implored him to abandon his quest, to reconsider his path of vengeance. However, Vishnudatt, unmoved by their entreaties, pressed on, his will unyielding.

From Indraloka, he ascended to Vishnuloka, the serene and omnipotent realm of Lord Vishnu. The tranquility of this divine plane, with its resplendent palaces and serene waters, belied the fierce determination that drove Vishnudatt. Here, too, the gods sought to dissuade him. Vishnu himself, with his boundless compassion and omniscient insight, attempted to steer Vishnudatt away from his destructive path. But Vishnudatt's resolve was steadfast. He was not swayed by their pleas, his mind was singularly focused on his mission.

Realizing that persuasion was futile, Vishnudatt turned his attention to the malevolent beings that inhabited the interstitial spaces between realms. As he ascended through the realms, he encountered a host of malevolent entities—Rakshasas, Pishachas, Bhutas, and Asuras. These beings, embodiments of chaos and darkness, initially confronted him with their inherent ferocity. Yet,

Vishnudatt, with his mastery of arcane knowledge and divine mantras, subjugated them.

The Rakshasas, with their immense strength and ferocity, became his vanguard, a terrifying force that swore allegiance to him. The Pishachas, spirits of the restless dead, offered their knowledge of the hidden realms and dark rituals. Bhutas, ghostly apparitions, and Asuras, ancient adversaries of the gods, all fell under his dominion, compelled by the sheer force of his spiritual might. Each creature, whether a nightmarish Rakshasa or a spectral Pishacha, was bound to his will, their powers amalgamating into his own.

As Vishnudatt continued his ascent, the ethereal presence of his Aghori mentor remained a constant guide. In the spiritual plane, the Aghori's form was a luminous specter, a beacon of ancient wisdom and esoteric knowledge. His guidance was both silent and profound, steering Vishnudatt through the labyrinthine pathways of the celestial realms.

The journey was arduous, each realm presenting its challenges and trials. Yet, Vishnudatt's resolve was unwavering. His samadhi deepened, his consciousness expanding beyond the confines of the known universe. The culmination of his journey was nearing—Shiva Loka, the ultimate destination.

As he approached the threshold of Shiva Loka, the very air seemed to vibrate with an omnipotent energy. This was the realm of the Destroyer, the embodiment of both creation and annihilation. Vishnudatt, now a formidable force in his own right, stood at the precipice

CHAPTER SIXTEEN

The Final Destination

As Vishnudatt approached the threshold of Shiva Loka, the very atmosphere seemed to tremble with an omnipotent energy. This was the realm of the Destroyer, a place where creation and annihilation wove their eternal dance. Vishnudatt, now a formidable force with newfound divine knowledge, stood at the edge of this sacred dominion.

Shiva Loka was an otherworldly expanse, an ethereal valley blanketed in unblemished snow, where silence reigned supreme and serenity enveloped everything. The valley was cradled by towering peaks that seemed to reach out and touch the clouds. At its heart stood the majestic Mount Kailash, an awe-inspiring monolith that rose high into the sky. The mountain's summit was bathed in a celestial radiance emanating from Lord Shiva himself. His divine form, seated in profound meditation, exuded an aura of tranquility and boundless wisdom, his eyes closed in eternal contemplation.

In the shadowed recesses of Mount Kailash, a cave cradled Ma Parvati in her peaceful slumber. The cave's interior was adorned with delicate icicles that sparkled like diamonds, catching the soft, celestial light filtering through the cave's entrance. Her presence imbued the cool, serene environment with a nurturing warmth, symbolizing divine love and compassion.

As the morning sun ascended, its rays gently caressed the peaks, casting a golden light over the snowy landscape. The sunlight danced across the valley, creating a dazzling spectacle of light and shadow. Mount Kailash stood as a sentinel to the south, while Lord Shiva, facing north, remained in his eternal meditation, untouched by the relentless passage of time.

Suddenly, Vishnudatt's voice shattered the profound silence. "Shiva!" he bellowed in a rage that echoed through the valley. Shiva, however, remained undisturbed, his meditative trance unbroken.

"Shiva! Awaken and address me!" Vishnudatt roared again, his fury palpable.

As Vishnudatt advanced, Nandi, the sacred cow, confronted him with eyes ablaze. "Who dares intrude upon this sacred realm? How do you trespass here?" Nandi demanded with an authoritative tone.

Without a word, Vishnudatt extended his hand, whispering an incantation. In an instant, a parshu materialized in his grasp. With a swift, precise motion, he struck Nandi on the head, and the cow collapsed, rendered unconscious in a single blow.

Ganesh and Kartikeya, observing from their vantage points on the neighboring peaks of Kailash, were astounded. The audacity of a mortal breaching Shiva Loka and incapacitating Nandi with such ease was beyond comprehension. They leaped down, their divine forms cutting through the air with determination.

"You have demonstrated your prowess," Kartikeya said, his voice resonant with authority, "but now leave this realm if you wish to retain your existence."

Vishnudatt, his arrogance unabated, scoffed. "I am not here for you, Skanda. Step aside."

Without hesitation, Kartikeya charged at Vishnudatt, his Sakthi Vel poised to strike. Ganesh followed suit, his resolve unwavering. Vishnudatt reacted with alacrity, summoning a blazing sword and a parshu. He parried their relentless attacks with expert precision, but it soon became apparent that defeating both gods would require more than mere strength.

Retreating strategically, Vishnudatt chanted mantras, conjuring a vast host of rakshasas and asuras. The battlefield was soon teeming with these malevolent entities. Ganesh and Kartikeya, undaunted, began to combat the horde with divine ferocity, their movements a blur of celestial power.

Seizing the opportunity amid the chaos, Vishnudatt sprinted toward Shiva, his resolve steely. As he chanted more mantras, a bow, and a flaming arrow materialized in his hands. He aimed at Shiva's solar plexus and released the arrow, his belief in its success unwavering.

The arrow hurtled through the air, its trajectory straight and true. As it neared Shiva's chest, Shiva's Trishul, levitating beside him, intervened. The arrow, imbued with immense power, pierced the damru on the Trishul. The resulting crack unleashed a cataclysmic shockwave that rippled through the Lok, jolting Shiva from his meditation.

In the midst of this divine turmoil, Ganesh found himself besieged by an ever-expanding army of Raktbeej. Each drop of blood that spilled from the severed head of Raktbeej gave rise to new demons, creating an overwhelming onslaught. In a moment of desperation, Ganesh cried out, "Maa!"

CHAPTER SEVENTEEN

THE KAAL AND THE KAALI

The primordial scream seemed to tear through the very fabric of reality. From the shadowed depths of the cave where Ma Parvati lay in tranquil slumber, a forceful, guttural cry erupted—Kali Ma's roar. It was a celestial tempest, a ferocious, otherworldly sound that resonated through the marrow of existence itself. This was no mere noise; it was a cosmic manifestation, an audible declaration of her immense and unfathomable power that made the heavens shudder and the earth tremble beneath its intensity.

Kali Ma emerged from the cave, her dark, formidable figure cutting through the snowy landscape with an aura of relentless dominion. Her skin was an inky black, a deep void against which the blood-red tongue of her scream stood out starkly. Her eyes blazed with a fierce, unyielding light, a penetrating glare that commanded immediate attention and absolute reverence. Around her neck, a necklace of skulls clinked rhythmically, each skull a chilling testament to her sovereign control over death and rebirth.

Her presence was a potent embodiment of divine chaos, a palpable challenge to confront the deepest fears and recognize the primal forces that lay at the heart of existence. The entities, resolute in their defiance, continued their assault with grim determination. Kali Ma moved with a deadly, hypnotic grace, her multiple arms wielding symbols of her formidable power—a sword, a severed head, a lotus. She swirled around Ganesh in a frenzied dance of destruction, beheading countless Raktbeej with merciless efficiency. Her every motion was a whirlwind of divine fury, each movement consuming the blood before it could touch the ground.

As Vishnudatt witnessed this awe-inspiring display of divine might, he saw Shiva descend from Kailash. The very ground beneath Shiva seemed to yield to his divine weight, and his Trishul gleamed with celestial, radiant energy. Now, two titans stood poised for a cataclysmic clash—one a god and the other a devout upasak—each prepared for a battle of mythic proportions.

As Vishnudatt saw Shiv, Lord Shiva stood as a striking embodiment of divine paradox. One side of his face exuded tranquil serenity—eyes partially closed, a gentle smile gracing his lips, and flowing hair adorned with delicate flowers. The hue of his skin was a calm, soothing blue.

In stark contrast, the other half of his visage hinted at restrained anger. His brow was slightly furrowed, and his eyes, though intense, were not blazing with fury but rather smoldering with a focused, simmering energy. This side of his face bore a fiery crimson tint, and his hair appeared more wild and disheveled.

The background mirrored this duality: serene blues and greens on one side, fiery reds and oranges on the other. Shiva's presence seamlessly blended peace with a latent intensity, embodying the balance between calm and power that defines his divine nature.

CHAPTER EIGHTEEN

ISHTA-DEVTA

As the confrontation between Vishnudatt and Shiva escalated, Vishnudatt began to chant ancient mantras with fervent intensity, his voice resonating through the air. Shiva, his patience waning, retaliated with unrelenting force. His Trishul became an instrument of divine wrath, striking Vishnudatt with a barrage of blows that seemed endless, each thrust and swing imbued with a celestial fury.

Vishnudatt, undeterred, continuously materialized astras from the depths of his arcane knowledge. However, each astral weapon shattered upon contact with Shiva's Trishul, their divine energy dissipating into the ether. The celestial duel continued for hours, the air crackling with the clash of divine energies. Despite Vishnudatt's relentless assault, all one thousand of his astras were obliterated, leaving him with nothing but the remaining fragments of his shattered arsenal.

Enraged by the futility of the struggle, Shiva's anger reached a boiling point. He began to levitate, his form rising above the ground as if defying gravity itself. With a deliberate motion, he extended his open palm forward. The Trishul, now an instrument of unimaginable power, began to rotate with a vertiginous speed. The Trishul's rotation created a vortex of sonic beams, each pulse of energy slicing through the air with an almost physical force.

Vishnudatt, caught in the relentless assault, materialized a shield in a desperate bid to protect himself. The shield shimmered and pulsed with protective energy, but the sonic beams hammered against it with unyielding ferocity, causing it to crack and splinter under tremendous pressure.

As the battle raged, Kali Ma, Kartikeya, and Ganesh were nearing the end of their struggle. The combined might of the three divine beings had nearly eradicated Vishnudatt's army of rakshasas and asuras. The battlefield, once a tumultuous sea of conflict, was now being cleared with each decisive blow from Kali Ma's fierce dance and Kartikeya and Ganesh's unwavering strikes.

Back at the heart of the clash, Shiva's fury showed no sign of abating. With a forceful gesture, he clenched his fist, bringing the Trishul to a halt. The immense power contained within the weapon surged once more, and with a mighty release, Shiva directed a colossal blast towards Vishnudatt. The energy was so potent that Vishnudatt's shield, which had been struggling against the sonic beams, disintegrated in a spectacular explosion of light and force.

The shockwave of the blast rippled across the valley, the sheer magnitude of the explosion echoing through the mountains. Vishnudatt, now vulnerable and exposed, stood amidst the debris of his shattered defenses, facing the unyielding wrath of the deity he had sought to challenge. The celestial battle reached a critical juncture, with the forces of divine power converging in a moment of unprecedented intensity.

As the confrontation reached its zenith, Vishnudatt, left with only his ultimate weapon—the Trishul—prepared for one final, desperate assault. He materialized the divine weapon with fierce resolve, its presence a testament to his formidable power. Charging at Shiva, Vishnudatt aimed the Trishul directly at Shiva's midsection. However, Shiva, with the effortless grace of a master, deflected the blow with a casual flick of his own Trishul, the weapons clashing with a resonant clang that echoed across the divine ground of Shiva Loka.

Undeterred, Vishnudatt adjusted his approach. He swung the Trishul from a different angle, but Shiva's defenses were impenetrable. Each strike was met with a counter that rendered Vishnudatt's efforts futile. In a bold maneuver, Vishnudatt leaped high into the air, holding the Trishul with both hands and aimed to strike from above. The height of his leap was dramatic, his form silhouetted against the turbulent skies.

But Shiva's response was swift and decisive. With a powerful motion, he blocked Vishnudatt's descending Trishul using the length of his weapon. In one fluid motion, Shiva drove Vishnudatt's weapon into the ground with a forceful slam. The divine ground beneath them trembled as Vishnudatt's Trishul was pinned, its celestial power unable to contend with Shiva's might.

Fury etched across his face, Shiva's anger surged. He unlocked his Trishul, pushing Vishnudatt's weapon further into the ground with a crushing force. The sheer weight of Shiva's divine might shatter Vishnudatt's weapon, sending shards of divine metal scattering across the battlefield.

Seizing the moment, Shiva spun his Trishul in a powerful clockwise arc, its edge slicing through the air with devastating precision. The blade slashed across Vishnudatt's torso, from his shoulder down to his hip, creating a deep, gaping wound that spilled blood and divine energy alike. The sheer force of the strike sent waves of pain coursing through Vishnudatt's body, and he screamed in agony, the sound reverberating through the valley. The gash was a grotesque fissure, raw and bleeding, a testament to Shiva's overwhelming power and the futility of Vishnudatt's defiance.

In a final, climactic show of power, Shiva hurled his Trishul into the air. As it spun and rotated, it ignited with ethereal flames, catching fire and crackling with otherworldly energy. Shiva leaped skyward, his ascent almost resembling flight, and grasped the flaming Trishul with a display of celestial might. As he caught the weapon, a profound transformation took place. Shiva's form morphed into Kaal Bhairav, the fearsome aspect of the divine, with the Trishul now crackling with lightning sparks.

Kaal Bhairav, the terrifying manifestation of Shiva, embodies the destructive and protective forces of the cosmos. His form is dark and fearsome, with eyes that blaze like infernal flames, a necklace of skulls adorning his neck, and a garland of severed heads hanging from his waist. He is the harbinger of time and death, a guardian of the cosmic order who dispels fear and evil.

The very nature of Shiva Loka was metamorphosed by this overwhelming display of power. The snow-covered expanse of the valley turned into a seething sea of magma and stone. The towering mountains, once serene, erupted into fiery volcanoes, their molten lava spewing into the sky. The once bright and serene sunlight was swallowed by dark, roiling clouds, which pulsated with bolts of lightning, casting an ominous, electrified glow across the battlefield. The tranquil beauty of the realm was replaced with a chaotic and primal landscape, reflecting the ferocity of the divine clash that had reached its apocalyptic climax.

CHAPTER NINETEEN

THE UNBORN CHILD

As Shiva transformed into Kaal Bhairav, the very essence of divine wrath and cosmic power manifested on the battlefield. His form expanded with a terrifying majesty, and the air thickened with the oppressive weight of his omnipotence. The onlookers were entranced, their gazes fixed in a blend of reverence and dread. Vishnudatt, wracked with pain from the gaping wound that marred his body, closed his eyes in a desperate attempt to escape the overwhelming agony. Shiva, now embodying the fierce Kaal Bhairav, grew four powerful arms and gripped his Trishul with a commanding grasp. His eyes blazed like twin infernos, promising divine judgment and relentless fury.

Kaal Bhairav's gaze was unwavering as he hurled his Trishul with unparalleled force. The weapon became a beacon of celestial fire, surrounded by searing flames and crackling lightning. The Trishul's trajectory was unstoppable, an embodiment of divine will and celestial might.

In that agonizing moment, Vishnudatt opened his eyes to witness the apocalyptic vision before him. The realization that his rage and quest for vengeance had blinded him hit him with the force of a thunderclap. The enormity of his mistakes, driven by unchecked anger, overwhelmed him. He collapsed, tears streaming down his face, surrendering to the realization of his folly.

At this critical juncture, another Trishul surged through the air, intercepting Kaal Bhairav's weapon mid-flight. The clash of the two divine Trishuls erupted in a blinding explosion of light and energy, redirecting the deadly trajectory. Kaal Bhairav's gaze followed the path of the deflecting Trishul, revealing Ma Parvati standing with serene authority, her divine aura shimmering with tranquility.

As Kaal Bhairav's terrifying form began to dissolve, Shiva descended gracefully from his lofty height. Extending his hand, he summoned his Trishul back to him. The divine weapon responded, flying through the air with a magnetic pull, wrapping its celestial energy around him and causing him to levitate just before he touched the ground.

Vishnudatt remained prostrate, still sobbing as he faced the stark reality of his misguided actions. Ma Parvati exchanged a knowing nod with Shiva, Ganesh, and Kartikeya, recognizing the resolution of this celestial drama. Shiva approached Vishnudatt with a presence of profound calm and compassion.

"Calm down, calm down, my child. Please," Shiva's voice was a soothing balm, gentle yet authoritative. "Your point was valid. You saw that for the past fifty lifetimes, you had been facing struggles in all of them. You engaged in extensive tantra sadhna across those lives, which is the reason for your exceptional spiritual growth in just fourteen years. Had you been patient a little longer, you would have understood the significance of your past lifetimes. In your 52nd lifetime, you were a king who ordered an assault on a Brahmin town, believing it harbored the betrayer of your kingdom. Instead of capturing the traitor, your soldiers, under your command, killed all the Brahmins, making you responsible for a thousand Brahmahatyas. You have been paying for that."

Vishnudatt, overwhelmed by Shiva's words and the depth of his realization, looked up with a heart heavy with remorse but beginning to find peace. The divine presence of Shiva and Parvati enveloped him, offering a path to redemption. The once-apocalyptic landscape of Shiva Loka was now a testament to divine grace, embodying the eternal interplay between destruction and creation, anger and forgiveness.

As Vishnudatt's thoughts wandered, an intrusive question emerged, driven by contemplation of his past. He turned to Shiva with a mixture of hope and apprehension. "Is any of my generation still alive?"

Shiva, his expression serene and knowing, affirmed Vishnudatt's inquiry with a simple nod. In an instant, Vishnudatt found himself surrounded by a luminous aura, his surroundings shifting rapidly. The divine energy transported him from the celestial realm to the earthly domain.

The once desolate wasteland of a dystopian future, marked by its barren expanses and ruined cities, was now transformed into the pristine paradise of Satyug. The bleak, scarred land gave way to a lush and vibrant world. The air was now crisp and fragrant, filled with the scent of blooming flowers. Forests stretched endlessly, teeming with life and vitality. Rivers flowed with crystalline clarity, their waters sparkling in the sunlight. Majestic mountains, now lush with verdant forests, framed the horizon, their peaks bathed in the warm glow of a resplendent sun.

Villages thrived in this age of righteousness, their inhabitants radiating joy and peace. Temples, tall and resplendent, echoed with chants of devotion, their spires reaching towards the heavens. Everywhere Vishnudatt looked, he saw the embodiment of dharma and prosperity, a stark contrast to the desolation he had known.

In the midst of this transformed world, Vishnudatt, overwhelmed by the profound beauty and peace, turned back to Shiva. The realization of his journey's purpose and the divine grace that had guided him filled him with a deep sense of gratitude.

As Vishnudatt marveled at the newfound serenity, he felt an intrusive thought take shape. "Is any of my generation still alive?" he asked.

Shiva, with a nod of affirmation, responded with a single, profound word: "Kalki." The name resonated with cosmic significance and divine promise. Vishnudatt absorbed the revelation in silence, the name echoing with the weight of destiny and the potential for new beginnings.

CHAPTER TWENTY

A NEW YUG?

As Vishnudatt marveled at the transformed world, his freckled body, marked by the trials of countless lifetimes, found renewed strength. With the aid of a sturdy staff, he rose to his feet, his form steady and resolute. Behind him, the grandeur of a magnificent kingdom unfolded, its towering spires and lush gardens a testament to the era of Satyug. The air was alive with the harmonious buzz of prosperity, a stark contrast to the desolate wasteland he had known.

He made his way toward the grand gates of the kingdom, their intricate designs gleaming in the golden light of the sun. As he approached, the gatekeeping guards, clad in resplendent armor, did not question his arrival or his past. Instead, they bowed deeply, their gestures filled with reverence and respect. The sight of these devout guardians acknowledging him with such deference was both humbling and affirming, a sign of the kingdom's alignment with divine will and the profound significance of his journey.

Perplexed by the warm reception, Vishnudatt walked towards a nearby house, his steps slow and deliberate. "Hello? Anyone here?" he called out, his voice raspy and weathered from years of silence.

A young boy emerged, running towards him with a shawl draped over his shoulders and a steaming cup of chai in hand. "Namaskar, Maha Guru! You finally woke up from your samadhi?!" the boy exclaimed, his eyes wide with awe.

"Maha Guru?!" Vishnudatt echoed, confusion evident in his voice.

"Yes, many believe that you gave Lord Kalki the power to fight Kali Purush," the boy explained with a mixture of reverence and excitement.

"Lord Kalki?" Vishnudatt questioned, a frown creasing his forehead. "No, Kalki is my son. He can be a king."

"Son?! He is an avatar of Bhagwan Vishnu!" the boy exclaimed, his eyes growing even wider.

The boy's enthusiasm was infectious, and he convinced Vishnudatt to accompany him to the palace. Vishnudatt, although intrigued and hopeful, made the boy promise not to reveal the truth about their relationship with Kalki. He would tell his son himself.

The journey to the palace took an arduous hour, the strain on Vishnudatt's aged body evident with each step. As they walked, the boy revealed that Vishnudatt had been in samadhi for a thousand years. Vishnudatt understood, reflecting on the notion that time flowed differently across realms and dimensions.

Arriving at the palace, Vishnudatt was awestruck by the city's splendor. The palace itself was a marvel of opulence, constructed entirely of pure gold. The seats for the ministers were fashioned from silver, while the emperor's throne gleamed with the brilliance of diamond.

As Kalki approached, he ran to Vishnudatt, embracing him with heartfelt gratitude. He believed that Vishnudatt's divine blessing had bestowed him with his powers. Vishnudatt, moved by the reunion and the warmth of his son's embrace, gently urged Kalki. "You can be a king, my son," he said with conviction. "Your destiny is greater than you realize. Embrace your role, for you have the strength and wisdom to lead."

Though Kalki was overwhelmed with emotion and attempted to persuade Vishnudatt to stay, the elder sage remained resolute. "I must go," Vishnudatt said gently, his voice laden with unspoken sorrow. "My journey is not yet complete."

With a final, lingering look at his son, Vishnudatt turned away from the palace, leaving behind the grandeur and the heartfelt pleas of Kalki. As he walked away, the sun began to set, casting long, golden shadows over the kingdom. Despite Kalki's desperate attempts to halt his departure, Vishnudatt continued onward, his figure gradually receding into the distance.

The serenity of the twilight was abruptly shattered when a Trishul, blazing with divine energy, descended from the sun. Vishnudatt turned in surprise, only to see the celestial weapon hurtling towards him with blinding speed. The Trishul struck with devastating precision, slicing through his body with an ease that spoke of its divine power.

Vishnudatt's eyes widened in shock and pain as the Trishul carved through him, the fiery force leaving a trail of destruction. His breath came in ragged gasps as he fell to the ground, the life draining from him. His final moments were marked by a mix of regret and acceptance, as he reflected on the destiny he had sought to fulfill.

In the dimming light, Vishnudatt's figure lay still on the earth, his body a testament to the sacrifices made in the name of redemption and divine will. The great kingdom continued its existence, unaware of the profound and tragic conclusion of the elder sage's journey.

CHAPTER TWENTY-ONE

A New Beginning or The Same End?

As Vishnudatt's corporeal form lay lifeless on the earth, his soul ascended beyond the mortal realm, carried on a current of divine energy. It was a transition marked by a serene, almost ethereal calm as his essence soared towards the realm of the gods. Upon reaching the hallowed grounds of Shiva Lok, Vishnudatt was enveloped in a radiant aura. Here, amidst the celestial splendor, Shiva welcomed him with a solemn nod. Vishnudatt's soul, now free from the confines of his earthly existence, was granted a new role in the divine hierarchy. He was transformed into a Gana, a celestial attendant of Lord Shiva, his spirit now one with the eternal dance of the divine.

Back in the vibrant kingdom, the aftermath of Vishnudatt's death rippled through the very fabric of existence. Kalki, reeling from the shock of his father's sudden demise, was overwhelmed by an inconsolable rage. The anguish of never having known his father's true identity and the bitter realization that he had been taken from him so abruptly ignited a fiery storm within him.

"I had no companion, no guide," Kalki roared, his voice reverberating through the palace and beyond. "And now that I have finally discovered who he was, you have taken him away!" The palace trembled with the force of his fury, the air crackling with an intense energy that seemed to distort reality itself.

The anger that coursed through Kalki was no ordinary rage; it was a primordial force, raw and untamed. From the depths of his seething emotions, a new avatar began to take shape, an entity forged from the very essence of his wrath. This avatar was unlike anything seen before—its form shifting and shimmering with an enigmatic power, an embodiment of anger and sorrow intertwined.

The palace, once a beacon of divine order, was now the birthplace of an unprecedented force. Maha Krishnkaleshwar emerged with an imposing, otherworldly presence. His form was both majestic and terrifying, adorned with six powerful arms that moved with an uncanny fluidity. Each arm bore a divine artifact: a Kamandalu, symbolizing purity and asceticism; a Kripal, a scepter of mercy; a Trishul, emblematic of Shiva's trident; a Gada, a mace of indomitable strength; and a Sudarshan Chakra, a disc of divine justice. His sixth arm was dedicated to wielding the cosmic forces that surged around him.

The avatar's body was enshrouded in serpents, their sinuous forms coiling around him in an ever-shifting dance of scales and hissing whispers. The serpents, representing the divine energy and protective power, accentuated the avatar's fearsome and awe-inspiring appearance.

The skies above roiled with unnatural darkness as Maha Krishnkaleshwar's fury reached its zenith. With a voice that resonated like the roar of a celestial storm, he unleashed a cataclysmic force. Opening his mouth, he conjured a black hole, a vortex of unrestrained destruction that began to devour everything in its path. The cosmic abyss swirled with an inky darkness, its gravitational pull so intense that it began to tear apart the very fabric of the universe.

Stars and planets were consumed in the gaping maw of the black hole, their light extinguished in an instant. Galaxies spiraled helplessly into the void, their once-majestic structures disintegrating into stardust and echoes of what once was. The universe, in all its vast and intricate splendor, was being obliterated by the sheer force of Maha Krishnkaleshwar's wrath.

As the black hole expanded, it cast an all-encompassing shadow across the cosmic expanse. The once-vibrant celestial realms were reduced to a realm of darkness and void, their existence fading into the infinite abyss. Maha Krishnkaleshwar, driven by the unrelenting storm within, watched as his divine rage dismantled the universe, leaving only the echoes of his immense power and the silence of cosmic annihilation.

The birth of Maha Krishnkaleshwar marked a pivotal moment in the eternal dance of creation and destruction, an embodiment of raw, unbridled fury that reshaped the very boundaries of existence. The universe, now a barren expanse of emptiness, bore witness to the terrifying majesty of the avatar who had been born from the ashes of a father's loss and a son's anguished rage.

In the cosmic ocean where Vishnu lay upon Sesh Naag, Ma Lakshmi's gaze was troubled. Brahma, who had needed to return to Vishnu's navel, had instead fallen into Ma Lakshmi's lap. His form was an empty shell, quickly dissipating into nothingness. Ma Lakshmi looked at Vishnu, her eyes reflecting both concern and confusion.

"This is not what was supposed to happen, with any of the universes" she said, her voice tinged with distress. "What transpired here to bring about such a consequence?"

Vishnu, his eyes filled with the depth of timeless wisdom, responded calmly, "In 2047, the world was on the verge of a new era where technology had seamlessly integrated into every aspect of human existence. A convergence of the digital and the divine was set in motion, a delicate balance that was disrupted by the events that unfolded."

Ma Lakshmi's eyes widened in understanding as Vishnu continued, weaving a narrative of how human advancements and divine plans had collided, creating ripples that affected the cosmic order in ways unforeseen. The fabric of reality had been strained, and the cosmic consequences were now playing out in a dramatic and unforeseen manner.

Glossary

Chiranjeevi: A term used in Hinduism to refer to beings who are immortal or long-lived. Notable figures include Ashwatthama and Hanuman.

Moksha: The ultimate liberation or freedom from the cycle of birth, death, and rebirth (samsara). It is the final spiritual goal in Hinduism and signifies the realization of one's unity with the divine.

Janeu: A sacred thread worn by Hindu males, symbolizing their initiation into the study of the Vedas and the acceptance of spiritual duties. It is typically worn over the left shoulder and under the right arm.

Mandir: A Hindu temple or place of worship where devotees gather to perform rituals, offer prayers, and seek blessings from deities.

Ishta-devta: The personal deity or preferred god worshipped by an individual. This deity holds special significance for the devotee, who may perform rituals and offer prayers specifically to this deity.

Aghori: A sect of Hindu ascetics known for their unconventional and extreme practices. They seek to transcend societal norms and achieve spiritual enlightenment through rituals that often defy conventional religious boundaries.

Samshan ghat: A cremation ground or cemetery in Hindu tradition. It is considered a place where the final rites are performed, and where the cycle of birth and death is symbolically addressed.

Tantra: An esoteric tradition in Hinduism and Buddhism that emphasizes ritual practices, meditation, and the use of mantras and yantras to achieve spiritual goals. It involves a complex system of techniques aimed at spiritual awakening.

Tantra diksha: The initiation into Tantra practices. This involves receiving sacred teachings and rituals from a qualified guru, and is considered a critical step in the study and practice of

Tantra.

Tantra marg: The path or approach followed in Tantra, characterized by the use of specific rituals, mantras, and meditation techniques aimed at achieving spiritual goals.

Abhicharkriya: A term referring to the practice of black magic or sorcery, often intended to cause harm or influence others through occult means.

Kaal Bhairav Ashtakam: A set of eight verses dedicated to Kaal Bhairav, a fierce aspect of Lord Shiva. These hymns are recited for protection and spiritual strength.

Aghor-diksha: The initiation into the Aghori tradition involves accepting its practices and philosophies under the guidance of an Aghori guru.

Sadhna: The practice of spiritual discipline or devotion aimed at achieving a particular spiritual goal or realization. It often involves meditation, prayer, and ritual.

Naam jaap: The practice of chanting or repeating the name of a deity or divine entity as a form of devotion and meditation.

Sadhaks: Practitioners or devotees who engage in spiritual practices and disciplines to achieve spiritual goals. They are often dedicated to their path of self-realization.

Upasakas: Worshippers or devotees who regularly engage in rituals, prayers, and meditative practices to honor and seek blessings from a specific deity.

Anushthan: A specific ritual or observance performed with devotion and discipline, often undertaken to fulfill a vow or seek divine blessings.

Havan: A Vedic ritual of offering oblations into a sacred fire, accompanied by chanting mantras. It is performed to invoke divine blessings and purify the surroundings.

Gotra: A lineage or ancestral clan in Hindu society. It denotes the family heritage and is important in determining the social and ritual identity of individuals.

Sadhu: A holy man or ascetic who has renounced worldly life in pursuit of spiritual goals. Sadhus often live a life of simplicity and devotion.

Rudraksha mala: A sacred rosary made of Rudraksha seeds, used in meditation and prayer. It is believed to have spiritual significance and benefits for the practitioner.

Samagri: The collection of ritual materials or offerings used in Hindu ceremonies and pujas. It typically includes items like flowers, incense, and food offerings.

Ghee: Clarified butter used in Hindu rituals, cooking, and offerings. It is considered pure and auspicious and plays a significant role in various religious practices.

Darshan: The act of seeing and being seen by a deity or holy figure. It is a significant aspect of Hindu worship, involving both the physical act of viewing and the spiritual connection.

Raksha dhaga: A protective thread or cord, often tied around the wrist during religious ceremonies or rituals for safeguarding and invoking blessings.

Kundali: An astrological chart or horoscope in Hindu tradition, depicting the positions of celestial bodies at the time of a person's birth. It is used for predicting future events and understanding one's destiny.

Adesh: A command or divine instruction, often given by a guru or deity, guiding the devotee in their spiritual practice or life decisions.

Beej mantra: A seed mantra, which is a short, potent syllable or phrase with profound spiritual significance. It is used in meditation and rituals to invoke specific energies or deities.

Mantra: A sacred sound, word, or phrase repeated during meditation or rituals to invoke spiritual power, focus the mind, and achieve higher states of consciousness.

Krishna Paksha Ashtmi: The eighth day of the dark fortnight (Krishna Paksha) in the Hindu lunar calendar, considered auspicious for certain rituals and worship.

Bhairav: A fierce and powerful aspect of Lord Shiva, representing protection, destruction of evil, and the transcendence of worldly illusions.

Ma Kaali: The goddess Kali, a fierce and transformative deity associated with destruction, liberation, and the dynamic forces of the universe.

Ma Kamakhya: A prominent goddess of the Shakta tradition, revered for her association with fertility, power, and the tantric practices of Assam.

Lord Hanuman: A revered deity known for his strength, devotion, and unwavering loyalty to Lord Rama. He is a symbol of courage and devotion in Hindu mythology.

Lord Parshuram: is a legendary sage and Vishnu avatar known for his warrior skills and role in various mythological stories. He is associated with the preservation of dharma.

Astras: Divine weapons mentioned in Hindu scriptures, bestowed upon gods and heroes, and used in cosmic battles. Each astra has specific powers and effects.

Shashtras: Ancient scriptures or treatises that provide guidance on various aspects of life, including ethics, law, and ritual practice. They encompass a broad range of texts in Hindu tradition.

Ma Tara: A fierce goddess in the Shakta tradition, revered as a form of the divine feminine energy and associated with protection and compassion.

Ghat: A series of steps leading down to a river or a sacred body of water, commonly used for religious ceremonies and rituals.

Tara-Pith: A sacred site or temple dedicated to the goddess Tara, an important deity in the Shakta tradition known for her protective and nurturing qualities.

Samadhi: A state of deep meditative absorption and spiritual enlightenment where the individual self merges with the universal consciousness.

Padmasana: The lotus position, a cross-legged sitting posture used in meditation and yoga to promote stability, concentration, and spiritual growth.

Dhuni: A sacred fire or flame used in rituals, symbolizing the divine presence and the purification of offerings. It is often associated with Aghori practices.

Rakshas: Demonic beings or malevolent spirits in Hindu mythology, often portrayed as obstructing or challenging divine and righteous forces.

Asurs: A race of powerful beings in Hindu mythology, often depicted as adversaries of the gods. They are typically associated with chaos and darkness.

Pishach: Malevolent spirits or ghosts in Hindu tradition, known for causing harm or disturbances. They are often linked with dark magic and occult practices.

Bhoot: Spirits of the deceased or ghosts that linger in the earthly realm, often associated with unsettled issues or unfinished business.

Mount Kailash: A sacred mountain in Tibet, revered as the abode of Lord Shiva. It is a significant pilgrimage site in Hinduism.

Nandi: The sacred cow and mount of Lord Shiva, often depicted as a companion and guardian. Nandi is associated with devotion and strength.

Ganesh: The elephant-headed deity known as the remover of obstacles and the god of wisdom, intellect, and new beginnings.

Kartikeya: The son of Lord Shiva and Parvati, known as the god of war and victory. He is also associated with leadership and protection.

Skanda: Another name for Kartikeya, emphasizing his role as the leader of the celestial armies and the divine warrior.

Sakthi vel: The divine spear associated with the lord Skanda. Symbolizing power and the destruction of evil forces.

Parshu: An axe or cleaver, often associated with the deity Parashurama, symbolizing strength and the cutting away of ignorance.

Trishul: A trident wielded by Lord Shiva, symbolizing the three aspects of divine power: creation, preservation, and destruction.

Lok: Worlds or realms in Hindu cosmology, often referring to the various planes of existence within the universe.

Raktbeej: A demon in Hindu mythology whose blood gave rise to more demons with each drop spilled. He was defeated by the goddess Kali.

Satyug: The age of truth or the first Yuga in Hindu cosmology, characterized by righteousness, virtue, and moral integrity.

Tretayug: The second Yuga in Hindu cosmology, marked by the decline of righteousness and the beginning of human imperfections.

Dwaparyug: The third Yuga in Hindu cosmology, characterized by further deterioration of moral values and increased conflict.

Kaliyug: The current Yuga in Hindu cosmology, marked by widespread corruption, moral decline, and the predominance of chaos and ignorance.

Chai: A term commonly used for tea in South Asia, often enjoyed as a daily beverage and a symbol of hospitality.

Lord Kalki: The prophesied future incarnation of Vishnu, who is expected to appear at the end of the current Kaliyug to restore righteousness and end the era of darkness.

Kali purush: The personification of time and the destructive force associated with the end of an era. Often linked with the destructive aspects of the divine.

Guru Vyaas: The revered sage Vyas, who is credited with composing the Mahabharata and compiling the Vedas. He is a central figure in Hindu tradition and wisdom.

Bhagwan: A term used to denote a deity or divine being, often used with reverence to refer to a god or revered spiritual teacher.

Gana: Divine beings or attendants in the retinue of Lord Shiva, often depicted as followers or servants of the deity.

Maha KrishnKaleshwar: A fictional transcendent, cosmic deity embodying the divine essence of both Krishna and Kaleshwar. This awe-inspiring being is a radiant, multi-dimensional force of celestial power and grace, seamlessly blending Krishna's playful charisma with Kaleshwar's formidable protection. Maha KrishnKaleshwar is envisioned as a mesmerizing entity that harmonizes the cosmic dance of creation and destruction, captivating with its boundless creativity and divine splendor.

Kamandalu: A sacred water vessel used by ascetics and sadhus, symbolizing purity and the divine essence of water. It is often used in rituals and spiritual practices.

Kripal: A term denoting compassion or benevolence, often used to describe a divine being or holy figure known for their merciful nature.

Gada: A mace or club, often wielded by deities such as Lord Vishnu and Hanuman, symbolizing strength and authority.

Sudarshan Chakra: A divine discus wielded by Lord Vishnu, representing the power of time and the destruction of evil. It is a symbol of cosmic order and divine protection.

Seshnag: A multi-headed serpent associated with Lord Vishnu, who serves as his bed and supports him in the cosmic ocean. Seshnag represents eternal time and the cycle of creation.

Ma Lakshmi: The goddess of wealth, prosperity, and abundance. She is revered as a source of fortune and success and is often depicted with symbols of prosperity.

Lord Vishnu: One of the principal deities of Hinduism, known as the preserver and protector of the universe. He is associated with maintaining cosmic order and righteousness.

Lord Brahma:The creator deity in Hinduism, responsible for the creation of the universe and all living beings. He is part of the trinity (Trimurti) along with Vishnu and Shiva.

Ma Parvati: The goddess of fertility, love, and devotion, and the consort of Lord Shiva. She is revered as the mother of Ganesha and Kartikeya.

Lord Shiv: A principal deity in Hinduism, known as the destroyer and transformer within the Trimurti. He represents the cosmic forces of creation, preservation, and destruction.

Lord Indra: The king of the gods and ruler of the heavens in Hindu mythology. He is associated with rain, thunderstorms, and warfare.

www.ingramcontent.com/pod-product-compliance
Lightning Source LLC
LaVergne TN
LVHW091519200926
848483LV00002B/252
* 9 7 9 8 8 9 5 1 9 9 3 6 7 *